the
LONG
ROAD
HOME
Return of Omohafe

WEST HAND

To order additional copies of this book, contact:
Xlibris
844-714-8691
www.Xlibris.com
Orders@Xlibris.com

ISBN: Softcover   978-1-6698-6508-7
           EBook   978-1-6698-6509-4

Print information available on the last page

Rev. date: 01/31/2023

CONTENTS

1
CHAPTER

The Glorious Omohafe

Sky and Ocean had their gazes fixed upon the magnificent sky above their head. It looked like a painting Sky once saw in a shop she visited with her parents once. The colors in the sky were fascinating. It seemed like a desert of sand hovering above the heads and was beautifully made of a mixture of elegant purple and bright orange. The stars were scattered all over the sky and shimmered brightly. They were not simply sparkling like stars on Earth. They sparkled like fireworks and looked radiant, like glowing flowers spread all over the sky.

"This is so beautiful, June; it looks magical up there," Sky said with eyes wide and fixed on the stars above.

"Yes, Sky, our world is just as beautiful as yours; look at those stars; are they not pretty?" June replied with a smile as he, too, was busy admiring the glorious sky.

"It is so pretty, Old Man Rain. Will you take me up there, please? Have you been there on that star, the green one?" Ocean asked June and pointed to one of the stars.

"Maybe someday Ocean, not right now. Let me show you around Omohafe first; I have a lot of other beautiful things to show you around here too. And remember, you must call me June now because that is my name here. No more Old Man Rain, okay?" June assured Ocean and patted her head.

"What is this flower called, June? This is very pretty." Sky called out to June, holding a flower in her hand. The flower bloomed open and closed as Sky tried to smell it. It tickled her nose, which made her giggle. It had the most refreshing fragrance Sky had experienced. A butterfly landed on a flower's petal on June's hand. It was as beautiful and fascinating as the flower itself.

"WOW! Ocean! Come here, look at this beautiful creature. I can see the light in its wings. How beautiful is that?" Sky exclaimed at the flower and the butterfly in her hand.

June turned in her direction and saw Ocean running toward June, giggling with the flower in one of her hands. She scratched her nose and lifted the flower to her nose - it tickled as it closed, and she laughed again. Light from the butterfly's wings beamed at Sky's face.

"I don't know what that flower is called, Sky. Your Father was the expert, and we all used to learn from him. This flower was your mother's favorite. How do you like the fragrance? Isn't it wonderful?" June told Sky and joined the two kids in the garden.

"Give it to me too, Sky; let me hold the butterfly too. It is a glowing butterfly; Please let me hold it." Sky yelped with excitement and joy and begged her sister to allow her to hold this beauty for a while.

"Sure, here, take it but be very careful, Ocean. We don't know if they bite, and they are too small too, don't hurt it," June carefully placed the flower in Ocean's open palm.

"Woah! These are so pretty and delicate, Sky; I wish we have them on earth, too; we will take a few when we go back. Is June okay if we take a few with us when we go back?" Ocean asks June and Sky pleasingly.

"Hmmm… let me think. Okay, you can take a few, but you have to promise you will take good care of them," June said after careful contemplation.

"I promise. Yayyy! Sky, you hear that we are allowed to take them back to Earth," Ocean exclaimed and hugged June tightly.

Suddenly she let go of June and fixed her gaze on the sky with no smile or excitement on her face. She looked sad. "What is it, Ocean? Are you not happy now? June said we could take it," Sky asked her when she saw her sister sad suddenly.

"I miss mommy and daddy; I miss them so much. I wish they were here with us; I would show daddy my new pet butterfly," Ocean said with a teary eye.

"Okay, girls, how about a little surprise? Close your eyes quickly, turn around, and don't look until I tell you to, okay?" June clapped his hands and turned the girl around.

"Okay, June," exclaimed the girls and quickly spun around with their backs towards June.

As soon as the girls looked away, June waved his hand in a circular motion whispering something under his breath. Once he was done with his spell, he joined the palms of his hands and stretched them wide apart, which opened a portal right in front of him. The swirling portal emitted blue and yellow light, and the girl's parents walked out of the portal. "You can open your eyes now, girl, look who it is!" June called on the girls, who stood still and motionless. The two girls instantly spun around and saw their parents standing in front of the portal. "Mommy, daddy," both the girls shouted in Unison and started running towards them.

Ocean was full of excitement. She ran quickly and jumped onto his father's lap, who caught her and hugged her tightly.

"Daddy!!" she shouted loudly, hugged her dad, and kissed him on his nose. "Oh, daddy, I missed you people so much; what took you so long."

"Daddy missed you too, munchkin. We were very far, you know; that is why it took us this much time," Daddy replied with a huge grin and hugged his daughter tightly.

"Here, daddy, look at this magical flower. It opens and closes continuously. Oh, where did the butterfly go?" she said as she opened her hand to show the beautiful flower.

"It is a beautiful Ocean; I am sure the butterfly will be here around somewhere, don't worry, we will find it," Daddy comforted Ocean, who looked concerned.

"It had lights in its wings, dad; it glowed, it was beautiful, and it didn't look like any others that we have in our garden on Earth; June said we can take a few from here," Ocean said hastily and enthusiastically.

"Yes, we will, Ocean, we surely will, Daddy said as she puts Ocean down on the ground again.

"This way to your dorms, if you want to get comfortable," June pointed to the doors to the left of them.

"We'll be back in a jiffy, kids; let us first slide into something more comfortable." Dad ran his hand through Ocean's hair and ruffled them up. She smiled radiantly and chirped, "Hurry, dad, then I'll show you around this place; the flowers in those gardens are fascinating, Dad." Her excitement was contagious, and dad ran quickly to the rooms, followed by mom.

After waiting for a moment, mom and dad came out of the rooms draped in beautiful long dresses. Dad wore a robe under which he was dressed in a fit and sleek black sweater and pajamas. The robe was brown in dark brown in color and looked like a cape. Dad fished out a shining stone from his pocket, checked it, and slid it back again.

Mom's robe was a dim white color with a hue of pink over it. It was laced with glittering pink ribbon and big glittering and fancy motifs that had the brightest beads on the back.

"Woah, mom! That is magnificent," Sky exclaimed with wide eyes and her palm sticking to her cheeks. "Where can I get one for me too? Can I get one too? Please?" she ran and circled around her mother and analyzed her mother's beautiful dress.

"You sure can; I'll get you made in your favorite purple color; how about that?" mom replied, seeing her daughter amazed by the dress.

"Is it a cape that you are wearing, dad? Can you fly?" Ocean looked at her father's robe curiously, trying to make her understand what it was.

"No, Ocean, it is just a robe; I cannot fly," he replied with a smile as he kneeled towards his daughter.

"What was that stone for, dad? The one you kept in your pocket, can I have it?" she asked, still curious.

"Oh, that?" Dad fished out the stone again, which had a little green light twinkling inside, and continued, "I am afraid I cannot let you have it. This little stone tells me if you are in trouble. When you are in trouble, this little light will turn red and bigger and brighter, and then I will know you are in trouble so that I can come to save you". He bumped her nose and smiled. "You will keep me safe, aren't you, daddy?" Ocean inquired.

"Always love," Dad replied and picked her up in his lap. "Thank you, daddy; I have to show a lot of things here, daddy. This place is amazing," she remarked, her pupils swelling with excitement.

"How about we do that tomorrow? Today we all are exhausted," June intervened. Ocean looked at Dad, who shrugged his shoulders and agreed. She had no option and agreed reluctantly.

June led all the parents and the girls to a room with small clouds floating in the center. "These are your beds, girl; your real parent made them, especially for you two with their special power. They are the most relaxing beds; your mother had them made especially for you two."

"I won't sleep in that; I will fall right through it," Ocean nervously said and pulled back a step.

"Yes, dad, they don't look very solid; we will fall, won't we?" Sky asked, looking at the beds with confusion. She, too, was concerned that they would fall through the translucent bed if they sat on it.

"Oh, don't worry, Ocean, you won't fall; I will catch you before you fall if that happens," Daddy assured Ocean and lifted her onto the bed.

To Ocean's surprise, the bed did not disappear from under him. Instead, she found the bed soft like one of her favorite toy bears.

Daddy lifted Sky and plopped her on the bed. Sky, too, found the bed cozy and immediately leaned back in it, enjoying the soft material under her.

"These beds are really fun, Sky; look how high I can jump on it," Ocean called as she playfully jumped on the bed.

Ocean laughed at Sky. Mom then told the kids to settle down as it was already too late and way past bedtime. They tucked both the children into their beds, wrapping them in quilts that Sky thought were made up of cotton candy. "Can I eat this? How will it taste? I wonder," she thought and smiled as the other kissed her goodbye. . The parent kissed the children goodbye one by one and left the room. Ocean slept with a smile on her face and her flower opening and closing in her palm. Sky was too excited to sleep, but the quilt and bed soon made her tired, and she was snoozing in no time.

2
CHAPTER

Sky and Ocean's History

Mother came into the room and pushed open the window allowing a rush of bright light to pour in and painting the room with fresh yellow light. Sky woke up and stretched her arms. She breathed in the refreshing air, enjoying the sweet smells wafting through the window from the garden outside.

"Morning, sleepyheads," mother greeted Sky as she gazed out the window at the birds singing outside and the remarkable butterflies that were buzzing out in the garden, jumping and hopping from flower to flower. "Out the bed now; breakfast is waiting for you guys already."

"Right away, Mom," Sky happily replied and jumped out of bed and slipped into her slippers. They were light as a feather, and Sky walked around the room enjoying the new soft and plush slippers for a while before going to brush her teeth.

"Is it morning already, momma?" Ocean asked as she sleepily rubbed her eyes and propped herself up in the bed. Her hair was ruffled, and a small lock of hair on her head was curled into a ball, making her look funny.

Mom giggled and picked her up, and stood her on the bed. "Yes, darling, it is morning already, and you need to get up and brush your teeth. Hurry up. Breakfast is ready, so up you go, come on," she planted a kiss on Ocean's cheek and brushed her hand through her hair. Ocean eased herself into her mother's arms, smiling naughtily, and Mom had to carry her to the bathroom to brush her teeth.

"Wakey! Wakey! Ladies! Breakfast is ready. Out your beds already, come on," Dad called out to the girls from the other room. Sweet fragrances wafted from the other room where dad had set out the table for breakfast. Sky and Ocean quickly brushed their teeth and dashed out of the room to see where the yummy smells came from. Ocean raced to Sky and sprung into Dad's open arms while Sky couldn't manage to reach and only got a hug.

"So many things, dad. Can I eat all of this?" Ocean asked inquisitively and excitedly; her eyes fixed on the plate of cookies with melting chocolate oozing out of one and a tall glass of milk next to it.

"Well, yes, of course, princess, we made this for you, all of this, Me, mom, and June," Dad replied, sliding Ocean into a chair.

"And those sandwiches, those are for me too, right?" Ocean asked as she immediately picked a cookie out of the bowl and extended her other hand toward the sandwich plate.

"Only if you eat the bowl of vegetables next to it, Ocean," Mom said before Dad could reply. Mom was in the room fixing a plate for Dad, who was cushioned on a chair right across the table.

"This orange juice smells delicious, Dad, and those muffins smell heavenly, too. Did you make them? I will take this and that bread with eggs," Sky said as she scanned the other table to see what other options she had. "That is a lot of food, Dad; we can't eat all of it at once," she exclaimed and jumped into the chair next to June. "Have some, June; what are you waiting for," Sky directed June as she handed out a plate to him.

"Well, since you both have been sleeping for two days, Mom and Dad thought it was better if they had all your favorites ready for breakfast."

"phuffft! What two days." Sky jerked forward in the seat she was comfortably sitting in an almost upchucked what she was eating.

"That is right, darling, you both have been asleep for two straight days now," mom confirmed with her and offered her a glass of water.

"But that is completely fine, Sky, don't worry; it is normal for everyone who visits Omohafe from the earth for the first time. Plus, the days and nights are shorter in Omohafe than on Earth, so it takes a little time to make sense of time around here. Don't worry," June smiled at her and comforted Sky, seeing that she was clearly alarmed and confused. Ocean was busy gobbling up as many sandwiches and cookies as she could possibly fit in her mouth.

"These are so yum, mom; why didn't you make like these back home?" Ocean mumbled as best as she could through her cookie stuffed mouth.

"Because we don't have the same ingredients as here, love," Mom replied to her excited daughter.

June picked a crucible fashioned out of the most exquisite Emerald Sky had seen. The crucible had animated carvings painted on the outside. The picture showed three golden cups going round and round the crucible.

"This was your real mother's favorite Goblet, Sky. Every morning your mother would make this juice from the fruits you see over there on that tree," June told Sky as he tilted the goblet and poured the fragrant, refreshing tea-pink juice into the round glass next to Sky's plate. He pointed to the densest tree that spanned out over the entire garden and was laden with purple fruit that Sky thought was a mixture of Brinjals and Oranges.

"Your father was an expert with trees and plants, and he planted that tree when he was just a kid your age, maybe even younger," June added as Sky fixed her eyes on the tree outside the window. By now, Ocean had eaten enough to pay attention to other things. She, too, had her widened eyes locked on the large tree and her jaw hanging in shock.

"That is old then, right?" she asked without ever slightly moving her eyes.

"That is correct," June agreed, smiled briefly, and sighed.

"Tell me about my parents June, my real parents; who were they, and where are they now? Why haven't they come to greet us yet?" Sky shot a series of questions at June, who was slumped in his chair, now looking tired and sad.

"Maybe they left us because they didn't love us, Sky," Ocean said with almost a trembling voice, "Maybe because we are always being naughty all the time," she added, looking at June with a tear rolling down her reddened cheek.

"That is not true at all, Ocean; your parents loved you more than anything, even more than we love you," Dad retorted and picked Ocean up from her chair and rested her on his lap.

"Then why did they abandon us, Dad?" Sky asked a bit angrily this time.

"They didn't abandon you, Sky; they had to leave you to save you from being killed," Mom replied before anyone else could.

Everyone was now still, and June dropped the sandwich she had in her hand on the plate.

"You already know that Eviler and his servants killed your parents, but your parents saved you by leaving you both under our care," Mom began as she pushed a chair next to Sky's and placed herself gently in it while resting her hands on Sky's shoulder. "Before they were killed, your parents left you with us and teleported us to earth to keep you safe. They also gave June the last cup he gave you when he visited you on earth. It is no ordinary cup, Sky. It contains a secret that can only be unraveled when all three cups are together. It is a secret to limitless powers, and your father wanted you to have those powers. That is what Ann is after, the cup. She wants it to be the most powerful being of Omohafe like your mother was. Your parents created us to protect you at all times. Your mother instructed us to bring you back only when you have grown enough, or else Ann will find you and inform her sons Ben and James about your whereabouts. The sons are an evil duo who want to kill you to get that golden cup. But after Eviler's death, Ann had grown restless, and there was no one that could stop her but you two. You must learn about your powers and master them to win against Ann. She is more treacherous than Eviler or anyone in all of Omohafe, and along with her sons, she is a threat to Omohafe and its people."

Mom wiped away a tear that trailed down Sky's cheek, and Ocean was listening intently too. "You and Ocean will have to fight against her, but first, you will have to collect the three cups to gain the limitless power your father hid away in the three cups. One of the cups is with the servant who killed Eviler after he killed your parents, and the other is with Ann."

"I am sorry, mom; I should never have doubted my parents," Sky rubbed the back of her hand on her cheek and kissed Mom's hand. "Where will I find this servant, Mom?"

"He is hiding my child, where exactly no one knows. But what I do know is that he is hiding somewhere across the treacherous Olive Mountains. Those mountains and the bridge on Tiberia Road that travelers have to cross to reach the mountains are legends and have seen many brave men perish. No ordinary man has been able to cross the bridge. Only the strongest at heart will be able to reach the mountains. The servant made it that far because he knew some secret passage, and he had powers granted to him by the plants your father gave him once. How will you do it alone without all of that?" Mom was terrified and looked inquisitively and with concern into Sky's eyes.

"She won't have to do it alone, Mom; I will go with her; that is what friends are for, right," June jumped out of his seat.

"But June, it might be dang.…" Sky tried to argue but was interjected by June.

"No, buts Sky, your parents were always there for me when I needed help and felt alone; plus, aren't we friends?"

"I will go too; I cannot be my only sister out there in danger alone," Ocean added as she climbed out of Dad's lap and joined her sister. "Well, if we are together, no one will be able to stop us, Mom," June said with a smile stretched from ear to ear.

"But you will have to promise me that you will be careful; your father made me promise that we will protect you at all costs," Dad tried to argue with visible concern.

"I promise Dad, don't worry, we will make it there," June assured Dad and hugged him tightly, throwing her hands around his waist and clutching as hard as she could. Dad kissed her forehead.

The day turned into night, and June, Sky, and Ocean were finally ready to leave. Dad and Mom came with Dad's favorite bag. "Here, princess, these are the things you might need on your way. Remember, be brave and stay together at all times."

"Yes, Dad, I promise. We will return with the cups, and I will make my parents proud."

"I am sure you will, princess," Dad said and wrapped all three of them in a bear hug. Ocean hugged Dad back. Mom kissed the children goodbye and made her promise that she would listen to her sister out there and they would look after each other. She promised and kissed her mother one last time.

The sky turned to June and Ocean, and seeing them ready gave them a thumbs up which. The two gave her a thumbs up in return, and she extended her palm and questioned them one last time, "Ready for an adventure?"

Ocean smiled at her sister and nodded as hard as she could, and rested her hand on her sister. June followed the gesture and, while resting his hand on top of Ocean's, exclaimed, "Ready when you are the boss."

The three cups on the crucible that were playing a game of merrygo-round on the Emerald crucible were now still and stood in line together, shining brightly and beautifully, bedazzling the room in their magical light.

3
CHAPTER

The Savior Servant

Here we are, Sky. The Olive mountains we have to cross lie across this forest, but I have no idea how to cross the forest. All I know is that there is a lake before the mountains that we'll have to cross. It is too dark for us to enter it." June, Sky, and Ocean stood in front of a dense forest. This was the first challenge they had to face. The forest was dark, and only the luminous butterflies fluttered around, hopping from one flower to another. Ocean lifted a foot to enter the woods, but June grabbed her, instantly stopping her in her footsteps. Just as she landed the foot forward, the tree separated, and a bit of a pathway appeared, but she stepped back as soon as June cautiously stopped her. Just when she retreated her footstep, the trees came together again, and the path disappeared again.

"Woah! Is this the "Helping Forest" mom often told us in her bedtime stories June," Sky looked at June, surprised.

"It is. But there might be surprises hiding in there, June; we have to be careful," June grabbed Ocean's bag to keep her from jumping into the dark forest.

"Oh, come on, June, I know of this forest; the trees will show us the path, mom told me in one of the stories, wait, let me show you," Sky assured June and took two steps into the forest. The trees parted, and the light illuminated a part of the path with her each step. "See, nothing to worry about; let's go," she called June and Ocean, gesturing for them to follow her. June grabbed hold of Ocean's hand and started following Sky's footsteps, and with every step they took, the path ahead illuminated as the trees parted. Ocean looked at the trees in awe as they parted and came together again and again. They were halfway across the forest when they reached a junction. The trees separated and showed three different routes for them to choose from. "What now, Sky? Which one should we go on?" Sky looked at her sister with concern and grabbed Ocean's hand with her free hand.

One path stretched out deep into the forest, and neither of them could see the other end of the path even though the trees were separated far apart for all the light to peek into the forest. Sky saw animals playing and birds flying across the track as far as she could. The second path was muddy and looked deserted. They could see swamp after swamp throughout the way as far as they could see. There was a big puddle of quicksand right in the middle, and the wet mud was bubbling. "That is so scary, Sky! Look, the mud is bubbling up there; do we really have to go through this track?" Ocean looked at Sky, scared and reluctant. "Oh, don't worry, Ocean, we are definitely not going through that one," Sky assured her frightened little sister. The third path was clean; at the end, two roads crisscrossed each other. "This one seems smooth; let's take this one," June sounded confident and leaped ahead. Sky quickly leaned forward and grabbed June's hand. "Wait, June, this might be a trap. We will get lost because we don't know where to go when we reach the crossroads. We will end up going round and round in this forest, and soon the sun will go down too."

"Then what do we do, Sky?" June asked, looking confused. "We go down the first one, it seems longer, but it is only a trick. I saw many animals and birds there. Living things depend on water; if there are animals, there must be a lake or some other source of water somewhere along the track. Didn't you say there will be a lake before the mountains?" Sky asked inquisitively. "There is," June replied patiently. "Then we are taking this one," Sky tightened her grip on Ocean's wrist and led the two of them onto the path. The trees on the other paths, too, closed again, and both courses disappeared into the darkness. The three of them walked cautiously at first but were soon lost in the beauty of the forest. There were plants and animals of every color. "Look, Sky, these flowers are sprinkling water; aren't they amazing," Ocean ran to a bush with many blue-colored flowers sitting on top of the brush like a crown. The flower sprinkled water from its center like a fountain. By now, Ocean had a whole bunch of flowers in her hand that she had plucked along the way. There was the blooming green one that opened and closed the red one that would send thorns shooting if someone plucked a petal, and the yellow one with brown edges that changed its fragrance every two hours. Ocean was as happy as a penguin collecting all the flowers and looking at the forest animals with wide-eyed bewilderment. "Be careful with those flowers Ocean; not all of them are safe; many of them might hurt you," June counseled Ocean while she ran to pick another flower.

After walking for a few more minutes, they reached a bridge with a stream running underneath. Every now and then, a fish would jump out of the water, do a somersault and splash back into the water. Ocean clapped with excitement every time a fish leaped out of the water. "Let us rest a little; we have a long journey ahead," Sky said as she dropped the backpack from her shoulder. June and Ocean followed her and did the same. She went to the fast-flowing stream and splashed a handful of water on her face. The water was cool and refreshing. Ocean tried to do the same, but her hands were too small, so June had to help her. They sat under the bridge and took out the lunch Mom had packed for their journey. "After we cross the Olive Mountains, there will be a dangerous bridge that we'll have to cross that lies across the Tiberia Road. Only a few people have crossed that bridge, Sky, and your father was one of them. We have to be careful about it," June informed as they ate lunch. "Ivsf'nt' theer any ovfer way!" Ocean asked innocently, sounding funny and speaking gibberish because of all the sandwiches she had stuffed in her mouth. "Well, we have to do it together; as long as we do it as a team, we will be able to do it," Sky persuaded them. "It is the most treacherous bridge, and it is guarded by the Brawny the eagle that is guarding the plant; it attacks anyone who tries to cross it," June added.

"I am sure we will come up with something," Sky assured but without much confidence.

"You know, kids, your father was an expert in Horticulture. He knew all the plants that could be found all over Omohafe, planted many plants in his garden, and knew all the powers and abilities these plants could grant to the users. He could use these plants to make medicine to heal the sick. He was the best in all of Omohafe." June told Sky and Ocean.

"I want to be like my dad June; I want to help the people of Omohafe too; I want to save our people from the Eviler's son and Ann," Sky replied with den day, but before that, you will have to master your powers, and for that, you have to consume the flower that you will find at the end of this journey, on the other side of the bridge at Tiberia Road," June informed Sky.

"I will do whatever it takes," Sky confirmed. The road ended, and the three of them now stood in front of a lake. The lake was peaceful and quiet. The birds chirping around the lake were melodious, and they could see the Olive mountains across the lake, which also reflected in the calm, unruffled lake. On their left, they found a small boat floating in the water with its paddle dipped halfway in. "Let's take that boat," June led the girls toward the ship. The three paddled the boat across the lake without any hassle and reached the mountain. "Let us tie our ropes together so we can catch anyone who falls," Sky ordered and looped a rope across Ocean's waist. She then continued with the same rope across June and, in the end, curled it around herself. "Ready?" she asked.

"Ready!" Ocean replied enthusiastically while June gave her a thumbs up.

They started climbing the mountain and started steady and smooth. Just when they were about to reach the top, the rock under Ocean's feet crumbled, and she slipped. June, trailing just behind her, fumbled too, but Sky could balance him in time. He firmed his feet on the rock again while Ocean dangled on the rope, screaming.

"Skkkkkyyyyy! Heelllllpppppp meeeeee!!," Ocean cried loudly, and the scream echoed across the mountain. June grabbed onto a protruding rock with one hand and pulled Ocean with the other. When she was within reach, Sky grabbed her by the collar, turned her around, and tugged her close so she could land her feet on the rocks next to her. Ocean instantly grabbed Sky and threw her arms around her waist. "It's okay, Ocean; we got you, don't worry!" Sky calmed her frightened little sister. They waited for Ocean to calm herself down. "You can hop onto my back, Ocean, and I will carry you to the top, just like we used to do back home, Come on!" Sky suggested.

June took Ocean and Sky's bag and helped Ocean climb her sister's back. After a hard and tiring climb, they reached the top. The view above was breathtaking. They could see clouds below their feet, and almost all of Omohafe was visible from the top. They rested for a while and then started their journey again. They came across a cave covered with vines on one end and an opening on the other. They peeked in, and the cave walls were lined with luminous shiny rocks. Sky pulled out a rock, and hurriedly, the three of them went out the other side. After walking for a few minutes, they came across a raggedy old wooden bridge.

"This is it, guys. We are here, right? This is the bridge on the Tiberia Road!?" Sky exclaimed. A few planks on the bridge were broken and a dusty old jacket flapped in the air. The sky looked down and couldn't see anything except white ashy clouds. "Hear, grab my hand Ocean and hold June's hand with the other, and no matter what, don't let go!" Sky explained to her sister.

Ocean and June nodded, looking scared and anxious. Sky led the three and stepped on the first plank. It creaked, and she waited with one foot on the plank for the creaking to stop. When she was sure that the plank wouldn't snap, she took another step. Slowly, the three moved, and the bridge started wobbling and shaking in the air. Suddenly, a shadow flew over them. The three froze right in the middle to see what it was. Suddenly a big bird with long talons appeared out of the smoky clouds and tried to grab one of them away. The three ducked, recovered, and started to run. The more they moved, the more the bridge wobbled. The bird returned and dived again. Ocean saw the two red eyes, and Sky quickly wrapped her under her arms. "Quick! Pass me your bag, Ocean!" she grabbed Ocean's backpack and pulled out the red flower. She tossed the flower to June. "Pull a petal when the hawk is near, and remember to lay low!" Sky instructed June. June, frightened and befuddled, could only wiggle his head in confirmation.

The hawk sailed up and then darted toward the three kids on the bridge. "Nowww!" Sky shouted, and the three ducked as the hawk's claw nearly missed June's backpack. June raised the flower and plucked a petal. Sharp pointy thorns darted out of the flower in every direction. Three thorns struck the giant wings of the bird, pulling out a few feathers. The hawk lost its balance and went spiraling down. It glided itself to safety and perched itself on the rock. "Go, go, go!" Sky yelled, and the three made a run to the other end. Ocean and June crossed the bridge carefully.

"Crrrrrraaaaaaccckkkk!"

The last plank snapped. "Jump, Sky, jump!" Ocean cried.

"Jump, Sky; I'll catch you! Don't look down; just jump," June called out.

Sky was terrified. The hawk screeched angrily from the rock and flapped its wings, trying to fly again, but failing; Sky took a step back and jumped as hard as she could. She nearly jumped in the distance, but her feet slipped at the edge. She was about to fall when June and Ocean grabbed her wrist and pulled hard. She leaped forward and came crashing on the two of them. Finally, she was safe.

The three of them got up and dusted themselves off. "Everybody okay?" Sky asked. "Yes, we are," Ocean and June replied in unison. "Thank God, let's move before Brawny comes at us again!" Sky instructed, and the three of them ran in the direction of the cave ahead.

They entered a dark cave and couldn't see a thing. Sky opened her bag pack and drew out the luminous rock. As soon as she took it out, a flock of bats fluttered, scaring the three. "Hello! Anyone here?" Sky called out. They saw a flame glowing in the dark, and a boy appeared in a torn sleeveless jacket and old pants. "Hello, are you Sky and Ocean?" the boy asked.

"Yes, we are; who are you?" Ocean answered defensively. "I am Wally; I was your father's servant," the boy replied. "I was waiting for you."

June took the stone from Sky and pointed it at the boy's face. "Yes, that is him," he assured and shook Wally's hand. "Here we are, Wally; what do you have for us?" Sky asked him.

"First, this plant that your father saved for you two will give you your powers. I had the golden cup that I stole from Ann. But I gave it to my friend Sarah because I thought Eviler's sons would catch me first. If Ben and James get their hands on that cup and the other two, they will have the power to control all of Omohafe."

"Where can we find Sarah?" June asked Wally. "In the forest between the sixth and seventh mountain of these Olive Mountains. You will have to cross a plain between your routes with hot geysers. Be careful, there are many geysers, and they are hot. You have to dodge them all before you reach the forest."

"Thank you, Wally. Thanks for your help. We have to leave now," Sky thanked Wally and shook his hand.

The three of them turned around and started leaving.

"Hey! can I join you guys? I can help; I know the place well," Wally asked humbly.

The three of them looked at each other and shrugged their shoulders. "Another teammate? Sure, why not?" Sky smiled and gestured for Wally to join them.

"Great!" Wally exclaimed. "Thank you!"

"Here, Wally, take this flower. Welcome to our team!" Ocean had her hand extended toward Wally with the Blue sprinkling flower in his hand. "Thank Ocean! Oh, the Sprinkle, it was one of your father's favorites," Wally smiled as he took the flower.

"We have to save Omohafe Wally, and we will need your help," Sky looked at him. "I will try my best to be of service, Sky. Now let's go save Omohafe." The four of them dashed out of the cave and disappeared in the cloud of smoke and mist as Brawny squawked from the rocks.

4

CHAPTER

Sarah and the Golden Cup

After the four of them were far enough not to hear Brawny squawking, they stopped and looked around. "So, where to now, Wally?" June asked. A small distance away, there was a big lake, and a mixture of fog and steam could be seen behind the lake, which blurred everything behind it. A thick layer of fog hung in the air over the mixture of steam and fog, and a sprinkle of water would jump behind the fog every now and then.

"That is where we need to go," Wally pointed to the place across the lake. The four walked to the lake and found large engraved rocks line going from one end of the lake to the other. June stepped on the rock and quickly hopped onto the other. "It is safe; come along." The other three followed with Sky at the end to make sure that Ocean and Wally crossed safely. Just when they were right in the middle of the lake, the first rock at the edge of the lake moved and immersed itself entirely into the water. Seeing the water, ripple the group stopped and turned around. They saw the rocks go down the water one by one. "What is going on?" Ocean remarked, confused and frightened. "Quick! Run, the rocks are sinking," Sky shouted.

"Look carefully, guy; these aren't rocked; look, they are giant turtles!" Wally exclaimed, "Faster, June, jump fast. We have to cross before all of them dive in!" he added. June picked up the pace and hopped quickly from one turtle to another; Wally, Ocean, and Sky followed, with Sky jumping just in time before the turtle moved. She slipped a couple of times but managed just fine. Everyone was almost on the other side except Sky.

There were three turtles lined in front of her, and all the others behind her had dived into the water. Since each turtle in the front was following the one behind, Sky thought she still had a chance, but suddenly two turtles that were directly in the front took a dip. She jumped hard, hoping she might land on the third but failed. She closed her eyes, hoping she would fall into the lake, but when she opened her eyes, she saw herself standing on the water. Her shoes barely touched the surface, but she wasn't sinking. "Woah, look, she isn't drowning!" Ocean exclaimed. "I think she can walk on water, and if she can do that, she can control water too; it is something your mom could do!" June said absently, shocked at

Sky's dramatics. "That is so exciting!" Wally added as the three of them stood watching Sky standing with both her feet on the water. Sky quickly but carefully tiptoed across the lake with a wide smile on her face. "Sheesh, that was close!" she laughed.

The four of them continued the journey, and after crossing a small patch of dense shrubs, they were standing right in the middle of the smoke and fog they saw from across the lake. There wasn't any water sprinkling about, so Ocean just walked straight ahead. She barely took three steps when suddenly water gushed out of a small hole in the ground and went flying high into the air before splashing all around them. The water was bubbling hot, and Ocean was just inches away from scalding herself. "Ocean!! Look out!!" Sky shouted and tugged Ocean back, grabbing her collar. Both fell into the shrub directly behind them. June helped both the girls up. "Are you okay?" he asked Ocean, who smiled and gave him a thumbs up, "I am fine, I am fine," she assured Sky and June.

"Look at the ground, guy; there are other holes, too," Wally pointed at the ground. "These are the geysers I told you about. Be extremely careful around the; II don't know when one sprouts up again!" he instructed. Sky got up and focused her eyes on the holes in the ground. She counted 32 holes lined up in 4 rows and eight columns in front of them. She saw that water sprouted from each hole alternatively. First, from the first, third, fifth, and seventh hole and then from the second, fourth, sixth, and eighth hole. "Ok, guys, we have to cross these geysers carefully. Listen, here is what we need to do. Look carefully. The water jumps out of these holes one by one. So we wait before hole number one, and once it stops spilling out water, hole number two there will start gushing water out. We have to wait for the water to stop and move just in time. The moment the water stops from one hole, we have to jump on it and move away from the one we are standing a because the moment it stops coming out from one hole, it will straightaway shoot out of one we already will be standing on, so be very quick. Got that?" Sky instructed them slowly, making sure they understood what she said. All three kids gulped and nodded as sweat trickled down their cheeks. "On my count of three, we jump! Ready?" she raised her fist and looked at the three intently. The three nodded again without saying a word and lined themselves in front of the holes. They waited for the water to gush out from the holes in front of them. Suddenly, steam rushed out of the holes like a shower, followed by water. As soon as the water stopped, Sky shouted, "Now!!" as they s jumped across the hole. The three kids copied her and jumped at her instructions. They were now in front of the second hole, which spewed hot water high into the air. They waited for it to stop, and as soon as it did, the four kids jumped across.

Carefully and smartly, they crossed the geyser dodging each hole together. "Woof, that was dangerous and thrilling,g was it not?" Wally asked as he wiped his forehead. "It sure was!" Ocean replied eagerly. They were busy congratulating each other when June heard a faint, slow whistle followed by a melodious hum.

"Do you guys hear that?" he asked curiously, raising his hands and gesturing for the three others to be quiet. "Hear what?" Ocean asked, alarmed and still. "The whistle and the light fluttering of the birds. Listen carefully," June said, freezing himself to make sure his movements didn't make any noise. Sky and Ocean listened carefully for a while and nodded. "Yes, I can hear it too!" Sky whispered, "but where is it coming from?" she added, turning slowly towards the mountains that stood like giant rocks in front of them. "It must be Sit is her song; she must be around here somewhere, but where is it coming from?" Wally informed the three kids and looked into the distance to try and find the source of the humming and whistling. "There, behind that large bush, a few birds just flew out from that wall behind that bush," Sky pointed towards a green bush that swayed left and right despite no wind at all. "But it is just a wall, Sky; there is nothing there," Ocean said as she looked toward the bush. "Yes, it seems like that to me too, Sky," June agreed with Ocean and looked inquisitively at Sky. "But I just saw a few birds flutter by into and out of that wall. Let's just give it a try," Sky replied in her defense and started walking towards the bush.

The three kids followed reluctantly and carefully, ensuring there were no more geysers or surprises. As they neared the bush, the whistling and humming grew louder and more precise. When they reached the bush, they didn't find anything at first. "See, there is nothing," June said, shrugging his shoulders disappointingly. "There, behind the bush near the ground, you guys see that it's a large hole there," Sky exclaimed excitedly, pointing at an opening in the wall behind the bush near the ground. "That is where the sound is coming from," she added as she ducked behind the bush and crawled towards the hole. The three others followed and entered the hole, which opened into a huge cave. "Oh wow," Ocean was wide-eyed and smiling. All kinds of birds and animals fluttered and ran around in the cave. "Sarah must be around here somewhere, she can talk to birds and animals, and if these animals are here, she must be around here too," Wally said, looking around the cave. "There, behind that rock in the middle of the cave, that is her right," Sky pointed at a little girl perched on a giant rock with birds sitting on both of her shoulders as she patted two furry animals that looked like raccoons. "Yes, that's her," Wally confirmed. "That is a wonderful song she is singing!" June remarked as they trotted towards the cave's center, carefully jumping from rock to rock. Listening to the sound of ruffling, the little girl stopped singing and quickly turned around. A giant bear that was striped like a zebra jumped in front of the kids and growled loudly. Other animals started wailing and growling and moving toward the four kids angrily. Ocean immediately hid behind Sky as the four came closer together, scared that the animals might attack them anytime now. "Stop! They are friends," Sarah's voice echoed through the cave. All the animals stopped immediately and stepped back. Sarah came and hugged each kid and hugged Wally tightly. "Good to see you are okay, Wally!" she exclaimed. "Hello Sky, hello Ocean, I am so happy to see you girls. I was wondering when you two would come. Your mom told me that you would one day visit Omohafe," she said as she hugged Sky and Ocean.

After the introduction, she waved his hands to two monkeys with horns and large round ears. The two monkeys ran to the far end of the cave and stopped in front of a large carved rock. Two big bears lifted the rock, and the monkey dragged a brightly shining golden cup from under the rock. The bears dropped the rock, echoing the cave with a loud thud. The monkeys brought the cup to where the kids were standing. "This is your parent's cup that Wally gave me for safekeeping. I was hiding in the forest near the lake, but Ann found me there and attacked me. I was saved by Hump there," she pointed to a large grey bear that had long hair all over her body. "She was accompanied by Ben and James oo, so I hid mill sundown and escaped the forest in the night using the turtles at the lake, and these birds told me about this cave and helped me hide," she continued.

"But now it is over," a hoarse voice hummed through the air in the cave, followed by a clickety-clack of footsteps. The kids turned around and saw Ben and James standing near the hole and a small group of evil kids standing behind them. "What are you guys doing here? How did you find us?" Wally gasped. The five kids came together in a close huddle. "Oh, we followed you here, we've been following you for a long time secretly, and now we will take what's ours," Ben retorted sharply in his hoarse voice. "And we will also kill both of these little girls!" James shouted in his raspy voice, pointing his sword toward the group and smirking. They both had their helmets resting on their stubby nose. "Go and bring that cup to me!" Ben ordered the group of kids. The kids marched to where Sky and her friends stood and surrounded them, pointing their sticks and spears at them.

5
CHAPTER

A Helping Stranger

You guys see that big rock?" Sarah murmured to the group as the evil boys cautiously moved toward them. "On my count of three, make a run for it; behind that rock is the cave's mouth!" Sky clutched the Golden cup close to her chest.

Sarah raised her hands and closed her eyes, and all the animals started squealing, roaring, and the bird started chirping loudly. Ben and James looked around defensively, and the evil boys stopped for a moment and looked around. "Get ready, guys, one, two, three!! Goooo!" Sarah shouted as animals and birds rushed towards the exit.

A big grizzly bear stampeded toward the evil boys, and the birds swarmed them. The bear trashed and tossed the group of evil boys that were in its way, and Ben and James quickly ducked behind a huge rock. The kids dashed towards the cave opening and rushed outside along with the birds and the animals while the approaching evil boys scuttled frantically for cover.

"Run as fast as you can, guys; come on, go, go, go!" Sky stopped at the cave's opening, making sure all the others ran out safely. They were barely a few feet away when they heard boots thumping on the ground behind them. June took a look behind and saw Ben and James marching towards them with their swords raised and their fists pumping, followed by the group of evil boys.

"There they are! Catch them before they cross the lake!" Ben shouted and started running faster.

"Which way, Wally?? Ocean asked as she ran, panting along with her elder sister.

"We have a lake right ahead of us; if we make it there, we might be able to lose them!" Wally exclaimed.

"I don't think we can outrun them; I don't see a boat to cross the lake with!" Sky shouted.

"We don't need a boat; we have you, remember?" June replied back, shouting to make sure he got heard over the loud thumping of the boots. "Oh yes! I do!" Sky replied and smiled as they reached the lake.

She quickly kneeled on the edge of the lake and placed her arm on the surface, and closed her eyes. The water started freezing.

She opened her eyes and was excited to see what she could do. She chuckled loudly, but as soon as the sound of the boots neared and grew louder, she focused harder, and the water started freezing faster.

She managed to freeze a wide strip of water that went all the way to the opposite edge of the lake. "Now, everybody! Run!" she called the group. Wally, June, Sarah, and Ocean bolted in that direction and quickly started crossing the lake. When all of them were on the ice safely and were almost halfway through, Sky got up and started running backward, making sure she could keep an eye on the approaching men and holding out her hand, using her powers to keep the ice frozen.

She had run across a few meters when Ben and James reached the lake. Ben jumped on the frozen ice and hopped on it to see if it was firm enough. When he was sure that the ice could hold his small army, he gestured for them to march forwards. Led by James, the team marched on the ice. Seeing them march on the ice, Sky got alarmed and scared. She looked back and saw the four kids standing across the edge of the lake, safely on the land. She turned around quickly and started running hard. She had stopped using her power, and the ice started to melt as she was now focused on just reaching across the lake.

She moved her feet as fast as she could, taking a peek behind every now and then. When Ben saw the ice was becoming slippery, he, too, picked up his pace and almost got his hand on Sky's collar. Sky arched forward, making sure Ben couldn't grab her shirt. The Sky was about ten steps away when Ben's finger tipped on Sky's collar, but just when he was about to grab her. A huge fish with wings plunged out of the water and slapped Ben on the face with its tail fin. Ben went splashing in the water, and Sky made a leap across to make sure that Ben didn't take her in the water along with him.

She landed flatly across the lake into the sand where the other four stood. She lifted her head and saw Sarah gesturing her hand toward the lake and saw the fish jumping in and out of the water on her command. "Thank you!" Sky said as she got up and quickly dusted herself up.

"Don't worry about it. We are a team. We have to work together. Are you okay?" Sarah asked Sky.

"Perfect! Let's go; The ice won't melt quickly. We have to keep running."

James and the evil kids quickly rush to save Ben and pull him out of the water. They had to fight the fish that would jump out of the water and attack them with their tail fins. The kids will turn around and run into the forest while the group following them is busy fighting the fish.

"Which way now, Wally?" June asked as they reached the middle of the dense forest.

"I don't know; I haven't been in this forest before. We might have taken a wrong turn somewhere," Wally replied nervously as he looked around the forest for a clue.

"So, are we lost?" Ocean asked, afraid and tiredly.

"No, we are not; we will figure out a way out of here too!" Sky replied quickly. "I am sure we will find a way out! Maybe it is this way," she added confidently.

The four kids followed her as she started walking forward. They walked about for quite some time but couldn't find an exit.

"I think we are going in circles; we have to stop and try to figure out a way first," Sarah said.

"Let me try if I could call a bird here that might guide us out of here," she added. The kids stopped and circled around Sarah. She twisted her lips and started whistling. The sound was melodious but musical. A tiny bird came fluttering from behind a tree and whistled, playing the same tune as Sarah. The four others listened silently as Sarah and the bird whistled one after another.

"The bird says we have to keep moving ahead in the same direction," Sarah was explaining to the kids when a spear came flying from behind them. The spear nearly missed the bird, which flew away behind the trees and disappeared. The kids turned around and saw Ben drenched in water, his hair wet and clumpy. His face was red with rage, and he stood looking at the kids with his lips contorted in disgust.

"I will make both of you my prisoners and will kill you as my parents killed yours once I have stolen your powers and will make all of Omohafe my slave!" he shouted. The evil boys jumped into action and attacked the group.

One attacked June at first, but June was quick enough to dodge the spear. He punched the evil kid with his left hand on his cheek. The kid was disgruntled by the punch and dropped the shield he had in his hand. June quickly grabbed the shield before the kid could lift it again and handed it to Ocean. Sky held the cup tightly in one hand and fought with Ben with a stick with her other hand.

Wally being huge in size, grabbed one of the evil kids, lifted him high over his head, and flung him over the other kids attacking the group. The kid landed on top of the others, and his feet knocked James on the head. James shuffled a little as his feet jumbled, and he fell over Ocean.

"Oww!" Ocean shrieked as James landed on her feet.

"Ocean!" Sarah shouted and ran toward her when one kid knocked her on her head with a shield from behind.

James quickly recovered and now stood over Ocean, who was dragging her feet and pushing her away from James. James held his sword over his head.

"Now I will kill you, you little brat!" he smirked and walked toward Ocean. He brought down the sword, but as soon as he was about to strike Ocean, his sword got stuck. Ocean had her hands stretched out in front of her and pointed with her palm in James's face. He tried again, but the sword would not move after a certain point. He turned around and saw a vine hanging from a tree wrapped around the sword's handle. Ocean moved her hand, and the vine moved with her hand.

"Woah!" she exclaimed as she experimented by moving her hand up and down and left and right and laughed as the vine and the sword moved in James's. "Looks like I can move plants and trees!" she called to herself.

"Oh, I've heard of this power from your parents! But never saw anyone use it. Not even your parents!" Wally said excitedly and surprised.

Ocean flung her hand to the left, which sent James flying to the left. She quickly moved her hands in circles, and many vines dropped from other trees and moved with her hands. She tangled one evil kid with a vine and gestured upward. The vine wrapped around the evil kid's feet and pulled him toward the top of the tree, and left him hanging upside down. Ocean picked up his sword and threw it in Sky's direction, who caught it and parried away Ben's attack immediately. "Attack the girl with the cup!" Ben shouted, and all the evil kids and James assembled around Sky.

A few turned around to fight off the rest of the kids in case they attacked. They slowly moved towards Sky. Ben reached her out and wrapped his fingers around the handle of the golden cup. Wally and Sarah rushed to save Sky but were knocked out by the kids. Two evil soldiers attacked and overpowered Wally despite his size and tied his hands with a vine, and another kicked Sarah on the feet when she tried to make a move knocking her unconscious as she fell and her hand thumped on the ground.

"Come close, and I will kill her!" Ben announced. June and Ocean stopped immediately, and Ocean dropped her hand.

A few evil kids who were entangled in the vines by Ocean came crashing on the ground. They quickly scuttled away and joined their team. Ben tugged at the cup hard, pulling it out of Sky's hand. He and James were admiring it when suddenly, a heavy hand landed on each of their shoulders. Before they could react, both got lifted and flung heavily across. When they landed on the ground, they saw the girls' parents standing firmly over them with Dad's fists lifted in front of him, ready for combat, and Mom's hands raised with her palms stretched open.

"Mom! Dad! Thank God you are here!" Ocean shouted in delight. The cup was tossed out of Ben's hand and landed in a bush.

"Dad! How did you find us?" Sky questioned happily and excitedly.

"We can always know where you are, kids. That is our superpower; we can sense when you are in danger and locate you. It is difficult in OmohafeOmohafe as our powers are a little weak here, but we did find you!" Mom replied enthusiastically, keeping her eyes fixed on Ben and James, who were still sprawled on the ground.

"Good! I was wondering when you two would show up. Now I won't have to find you two and kill you separately. Will save me time!" Ben laughed and picked himself up and dusted his armor.

He picked up his sword, and so did James. The kids came running and surrounded their king. The kids assembled, but Wally couldn't as he was tied to a tree with a vine.

"Until now, I was thinking of making you my slave, girls, but since you have given me so much trouble, I would go on to killing you without wasting any time!" Ben said sharply with a wicked smile on his face. "Give it your best shot, you murderer!" Sky replied angrily, locking his eyes with Ben. "Kill them, kill them all!!" Ben shouted as the group marched toward the kids and the parents.

Ben and James attacked Dad first and knocked him unconscious. Two evil kids overpowered Mom and cornered her. Ben and James then marched toward June, Sky, and Ocean.

"This is over now, kids, now you die, and I will end up ruling all of Omohafe!" Ben said as he moved toward the kids.

June jumped to the girls' defense and threw a punch in Ben's direction. Ben moved out of the way, and James bumped June with his sword's handle in the head. Sky picked up a sword from the ground and carefully moved towards Ben. James moved around and started walking in Ocean's direction. Sky swung her sword, but Ben blocked it with his and nimbly slashed Sky's arm in a counterattack.

James waited for Sky to attack him, and when she did, she dodged her and pushed her toward Sky. Both the sisters were on the ground. Seeing her arm bleed, Sky decided to help her sister up, but just as the sisters locked with fingers with each other, a loud bang surged through them and around the forest. A bright burst of blinding white light exploded from their hands, sending them and everyone standing flying across the forest. June gasped at the sight.

"Oh no, it can't be! Not yet!" he whispered to himself as he looked at the two girls on the floor in awe.

Confused and surprised, Ben and James picked themselves up. "This is the power your parents talked about. And I will steal it from you!" Ben said loudly.

Sky and Ocean were on the floor, weakened by what had happened. Before she could gather herself, Ben was already standing over her head with a mean smile on his face. He was an arm's length away from Sky, he raised his sword, but before it could strike her, it was blocked by a metallic clang of another sword.

Next to Ben, a man in a long cloak and a hood over his head stood, holding the sword in his stretched hand. No one could see the face under his hood. Ben gasped in surprise and fear and immediately swung his sword again. The man parried the strike again seamlessly. James joined his brother, and both attacked the man simultaneously, but the man held his ground and effortlessly fought them both. He ducked and spun, kicking both in the feet. He knocked James unconscious the moment he fell on the ground with his sword handle and then pointed the blade toward Ben. Ben sheepishly gathered himself, and the kids huddled around him. They lifted unconscious James over their shoulders. The man shooed them away.

Sky hurriedly went and pulled out the cup from the bush; June went and untied tally and splashed a little water from a puddle on the ground to wake Sarah up. Ocean quickly ran and checked up on Mom and Dad. She and mom shook Dad hard, who opened his eyes slowly. Sky checked up on everybody, and all of them gathered around Dad and Mom. Once everyone was found okay except for a few bruises here and there, they all turned around to look at the man who was walking away into the dense forest.

"Wait," Sky and Ocean shouted in unison, "Who are you?" they both added together. The man stopped, turned around, waited, and then turned back and walked away.

Sky couldn't see any of his facial features except one. Sky saw clearly that the man smiled.

6
CHAPTER

June's Secret

The strange man briskly and quickly walked away into the forest before Sky or Ocean could ask another question. Ocean thought of running behind her, but Sky grabbed her by the hand. "Don't follow strange men Ocean. We don't know who he was," She counseled Ocean.

"But he saved our life!" Ocean protested. "Maybe, but it seems like he doesn't want to be bothered. Let him be," Sky replied to her eager sister. After the strange man was gone, Mom checked up on the slash on Sky's arm. She hovered her hand over the gash that was bleeding, and a faint light emanated through her palm, instantly healing the wound. "Thank you, Mom!" Sky smiled. She inspected the golden cup she had in her hand. It was scratchless. "Any idea who the man was?" Sarah asked the group, her mind still groggy from the fighting. Everyone nodded a "No." "Wally?" she turned to where Wally was standing, rubbing his fists, trying to remove the marking left by the vines when he was tied. "Not a clue, haven't seen him before!" he replied.

"What was all that power and explosion, Dad? I didn't do it, and neither did Sky. It just happened, like a Boom!" Ocean inquired her father, stretching her hands in a circle to imitate an explosion. "I don't know, but I think June might have an answer to this." Can you explain what happened, June? Ocean is right. I didn't do what happened there. I didn't even know I could do something like that; it just happened!" Sky looked at June with curious eyes.

"It is a long-hidden secret, Sky! Your father made me promise I won't tell you about it until you both master your power. It is, it is…." June started speaking after a long sigh. He stopped and thought for a little while. "I think it is the right time, June; the fate of Omohafe is at stake, and we must know what is necessary, don't you think?" Sky asked her innocently. "Okay, okay, But you'll have to promise me you won't use it until you both have learned to control your power!" he looked at Sky and then at Ocean, who was listening to the conversation intently.

"We promise!" both replied in unison.

"It is called the Sibling bond of Superpower, and it is the deadliest combination of powers. It has been used on occasion and always ended in disaster. Only those who share the truest of bonds with each other can wield power. When two such power wielders join hands together, their powers combine, and together they can do many other things as the combination of the powers enhances their own powers and give them new abilities too." "They end in a disaster, you said. How and why, June?" Sky asked. By now, everyone was resting on the ground or a rock. Ocean using her powers, made a long bench from the wood barks for Mom and Dad to sit on.

"Yes, always. Because the power cannot be contained, it requires a very strong bond to keep the power surge within limits, and it requires a great amount of control too. There have been two occasions when the power was used, and both ended with death and destruction. The first time was when two of your great granduncles used them against Eviler's grandparents. Eviler's grandparents were the King and Queen of Omohafe, and they were cruel. They ruled Omohafe like tyrants, and no one could question them. Anyone who did they will punish by locking them up in prison, or they would drive them out of Omohafe into the dense forest that had all kinds of wild beasts. Your great granduncles couldn't take that and decided to end this once and for all. They attacked the castle with their small army of loyal followers, but they were outmatched. Their army was killed, and they were taken to Eviler's grandparents in chains as prisoners. The King and the Queen laughed and mocked them and told them that no one could rule Omohafe but they and their children and grandchildren, and they would now punish the families of the loyal followers for helping their uncles. That is when your uncles joined hands and caused the explosion. Uncle August had the power to emit energy blasts, and Uncle Drizzle could control and manipulate fire. The combined power caused the biggest explosion that was even heard on the outskirts of Omohafe. The explosion killed everyone in the Castle, along with your uncles. They died trying to save Omohafe from the tyrant King and Queen."

Sky and Ocean had tears rolling down their cheek. "What about the second time?" asked Sarah.

"The second time was when a brother and sister used the Sibling bonds of Superpower to fend off an army that attacked Omohafe. It was when your parents ruled Omohafe. Legend has it that an army from the neighboring planet invaded Omohafe. It was led by their king named Rot, who used to invade other planets and moons and made the people his slaves. He had killed many people in his conquest, and he aspired to be the most powerful warlord in the entire galaxy. He was very powerful and skilled himself, too, and so was the army he used. When he attacked Omohafe, our army fought bravely, and many men died fighting him. We had almost won the battle, but Eviler betrayed your father and his army and gave King Rot the directions of a secret passage in exchange for a share in his Kingdom. Rot marched toward the passage, but it was two young brothers and a sister who were the children of the guard that was posted on that passage who had died battling the enemy's army. They came to defend their father's post, and when they saw the army of Rot coming, they locked their hands together. The explosion vaporized and wiped out the entire army of King Rot and saved Omohafe and many other planets from a future invasion. The brother and the sister sacrificed their lives for Omohafe. Eviler was caught for his betrayal, but he broke out of prison and later killed his parents, and now his sons are trying to rule Omohafe. Even if it saved his kingdom, your father banned the use of the power and dedicated teachers to better learn the use of this power. He studied power for a long time and mastered control. One of the reasons he wanted to study plants was because he figured out a way to use the plants to control the powers."

"Then I promise I will master my powers and make sure Eviler's sons don't get away this time. We have to be prepared this time when they come." Sky said, wiping away her tears. "And this time, they will see what our powers can do!" Ocean said, sounding determined.

"Okay, kids, we have to return now! If I know them, they will be planning another attack soon," Dad said worriedly. "We have to rush home now as no one is safeguarding the throne right now. The group recollected themselves and came together in a circle. "June, will you?" Mom looked at June. "Of course," he replied and waved his hand in a circle and murmured a few words. A portal appeared in front of them that opened back into the garden of Sky and Ocean's home. All of them walked through the portal, with June entering it the last. An eviler kid that was lying unconscious on the ground opened his eyes as everyone left.

After three days, Dad gathered everyone in the garden. Wally was happy and excited to be back. "It is so good to be back here, Sky, your father and I have a lot of good memories here. He used to study under that tree you see there and taught me many things too. You are very much like your father," he pointed to the big tree in the center of the garden. He had a broad smile on his face.

"He was brave like you and helped others before himself too. What you did at the lake was heroic!" he said to Sky. "I didn't do much, Wally; you would have done the same; we made it out simply because we were a good team. If we do everything as a team, we win always have more chances of winning," she smiled back at Wally.

"Okay, children, we have assembled here the best teachers in Omohafe. They will teach you to use your powers and control them better, so let's begin." The kids lined themselves up in a line and stood in front of a group of men and women who were wearing long, bright robes. An elderly man came forward, hovering a few inches above the ground, and said, "Morning, kids! Let the classes begin" Everyone came forward. Everyone was there except June.

"Where is June?" Ocean whispered to Sky. "I don't know," she replied. Dad looked around and saw June sitting under the tree crouched. "June! Come on in, son!" Dad called him. "Coming!" he replied back.

"Should I tell them? or should I wait? How will they react? But I have to tell them someday; the sooner, the better, I guess" June was busy talking to himself. He was nervous and scared, and sweat trickled down from his temple. "Maybe not today, maybe in a few days' time, I will," he said as he got up and wiped his sweat. "We are not starting without you, June!" Sky called him out.

"I am coming!" he shouted back. "Okay, so it is decided; just a few days more, then I will tell them all!"

He dashed and joined the team and stood next to Sky. "Are you okay?" Sky asked him. "Perfect!" he said, "Let's begin, shall we?" he smiled at Sky and the teachers.

Printed in the United States
by Baker & Taylor Publisher Services